MANGA SHAKESPEARE®

MUCH ADO
ABOUT NOTHING

ADAPTED BY
RICHARD APPIGNANESI

ILLUSTRATED BY
EMMA VIECELI

Published by
SelfMadeHero
139-141 Pancras Road
London NW1 1UN
www.selfmadehero.com

This edition published 2017

Illustrator: Emma Vieceli
Text Adaptor: Richard Appignanesi
Designer: Andy Huckle
Textual Consultant: Nick de Somogyi
Publishing Director: Emma Hayley

ISBN: 978-0-9558169-6-3

10 9 8 7 6
Printed and bound in Slovenia

"When I said I would die a bachelor... I did not think I should live till I were married..."

Beatrice of Messina

"Stand I condemned
for pride and scorn
so much?"

Claudio of Florence, of Don Pedro's company

"That I love Hero, I feel!"

"Our watch have comprehended two auspicious persons…"

Dogberry, a foolish policeman

"Give them their charge!"

Verges, his deputy

I THINK THIS IS YOUR DAUGHTER.

HER MOTHER HATH MANY TIMES TOLD ME SO.

WERE YOU IN DOUBT, SIR, THAT YOU ASKED HER?

SIGNIOR BENEDICK, NO, FOR THEN WERE *YOU* A CHILD.

YOU HAVE IT FULL, BENEDICK. TRULY THE LADY FATHERS HERSELF.

SIGNIOR BENEDICK, NOBODY *MARKS* YOU.

BUT KEEP YOUR WAY, O' GOD'S NAME.

I AM DONE.

YOU ALWAYS END WITH A JADE'S TRICK.

I KNOW YOU OF OLD.

LEONATO HATH INVITED YOU ALL. WE SHALL STAY HERE A MONTH.

LET ME BID YOU WELCOME, MY LORD, BEING RECONCILED TO THE PRINCE, YOUR BROTHER.

I AM NOT A MAN OF MANY WORDS, BUT I THANK YOU.

21

THAT I LOVE HER, I FEEL.

THAT SHE IS WORTHY, I KNOW.

THAT I NEITHER FEEL HOW SHE SHOULD BE LOVED, NOR KNOW HOW SHE SHOULD BE WORTHY, IS THE OPINION THAT *FIRE* CANNOT MELT OUT OF ME.

I WILL DIE IN IT AT THE STAKE.

WELL, IF THOU EVER DOST FALL FROM THIS FAITH, THOU WILT PROVE A NOTABLE ARGUMENT.

IF I DO, HANG ME IN A BOTTLE LIKE A CAT AND SHOOT AT ME.

"IN TIME THE SAVAGE BULL DOTH BEAR THE YOKE."

IN THE MEANTIME, REPAIR TO LEONATO'S AND TELL HIM I WILL NOT FAIL HIM AT SUPPER.

I HAVE ALMOST ENOUGH IN ME FOR SUCH AN EMBASSAGE.

POINK

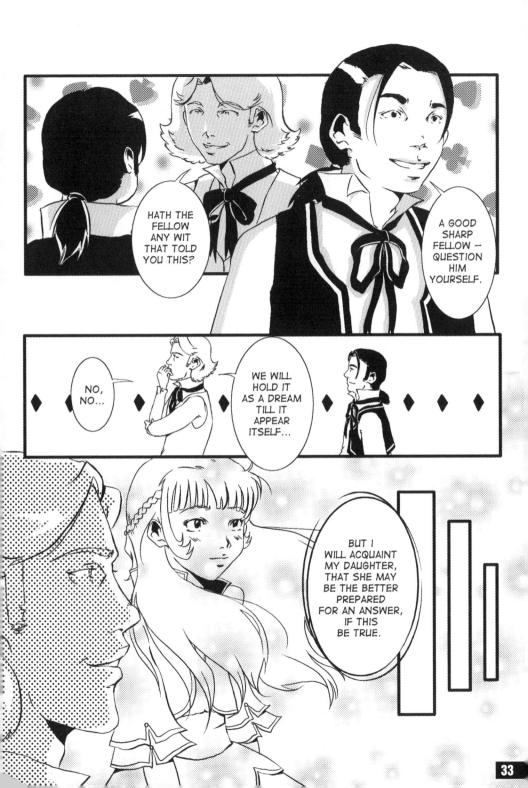

HATH THE FELLOW ANY WIT THAT TOLD YOU THIS?

A GOOD SHARP FELLOW — QUESTION HIM YOURSELF.

NO, NO...

WE WILL HOLD IT AS A DREAM TILL IT APPEAR ITSELF...

BUT I WILL ACQUAINT MY DAUGHTER, THAT SHE MAY BE THE BETTER PREPARED FOR AN ANSWER, IF THIS BE TRUE.

I HEARD IT AGREED THAT THE PRINCE SHOULD WOO HERO FOR HIMSELF...

AND, HAVING OBTAINED HER, GIVE HER TO COUNT CLAUDIO.

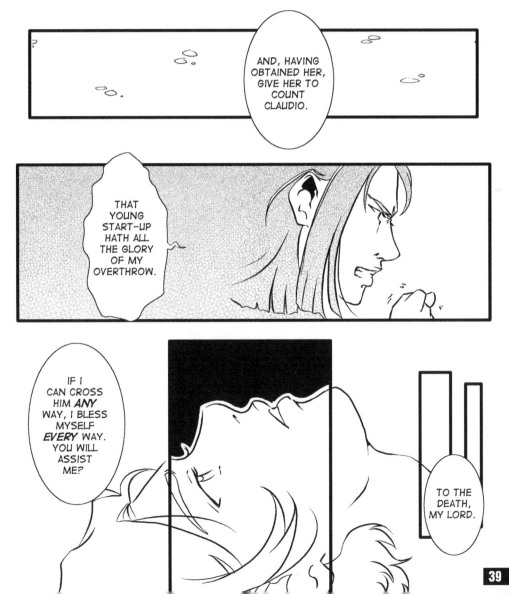

THAT YOUNG START-UP HATH ALL THE GLORY OF MY OVERTHROW.

IF I CAN CROSS HIM *ANY* WAY, I BLESS MYSELF *EVERY* WAY. YOU WILL ASSIST ME?

TO THE DEATH, MY LORD.

WAS NOT COUNT JOHN HERE AT SUPPER?

I SAW HIM NOT.

I NEVER CAN SEE HIM BUT I AM *HEART-BURNED* AN HOUR AFTER.

HE IS OF A VERY MELANCHOLY DISPOSITION.

IT IS MY COUSIN'S DUTY TO SAY "FATHER, AS IT PLEASE YOU."

BUT YET, LET HIM BE A HANDSOME FELLOW...

WELL, NIECE, I TRUST *YOU* WILL BE RULED BY YOUR FATHER.

OR MAKE ANOTHER CURTSY AND SAY "FATHER, AS IT PLEASE *ME*."

DAUGHTER, REMEMBER WHAT I TOLD YOU. IF THE PRINCE DO SOLICIT YOU IN THAT KIND, YOU KNOW YOUR ANSWER.

THE FAULT WILL BE IN THE MUSIC, COUSIN, IF YOU BE NOT WOOED IN GOOD TIME...

WOOING — WEDDING — REPENTANCE

och aye!

FOR WOOING, WEDDING AND REPENTING IS AS A SCOTCH JIG, A MEASURE AND A CINQUEPACE.

THE FIRST IS HOT AND HASTY LIKE A *SCOTCH JIG*...

THE WEDDING, MANNERLY, MODEST, AS A *MEASURE*...

AND THEN COMES REPENTANCE, AND WITH HIS BAD LEGS FALLS INTO THE *CINQUEPACE* FASTER AND FASTER...

TILL HE SINK INTO HIS *GRAVE*.

CLAP CLAP

!!!

bink

WILL YOU NOT TELL ME WHO YOU ARE?

NOT NOW.

THAT I WAS *DISDAINFUL* —

WELL... THIS WAS SIGNIOR *BENEDICK* THAT SAID SO.

WHAT'S HE?

WHY, HE IS THE PRINCE'S *JESTER*.

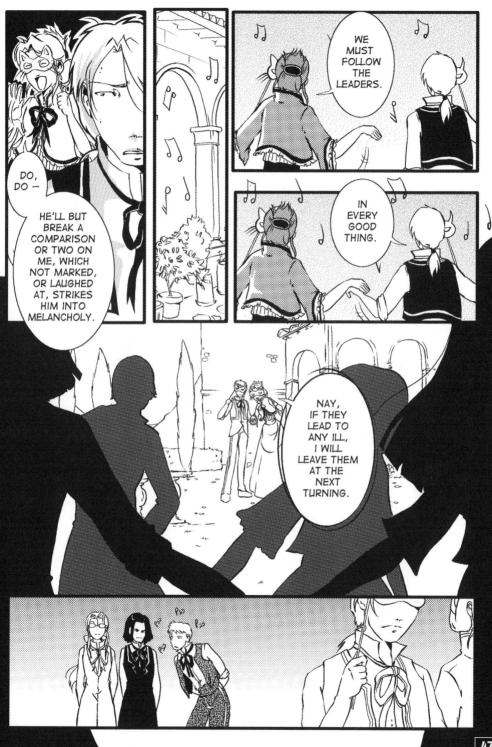

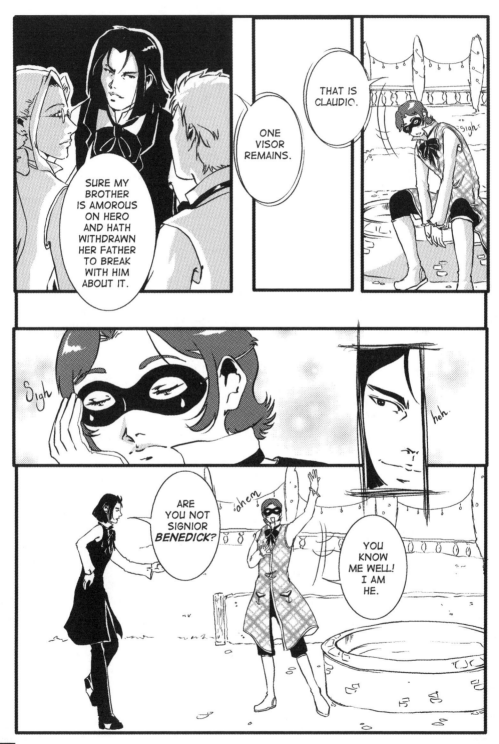

SIGNIOR, YOU ARE VERY NEAR MY BROTHER IN HIS *LOVE*.

HE IS ENAMOURED ON HERO.

I PRAY YOU, DISSUADE HIM FROM HER. SHE IS NO EQUAL FOR HIS BIRTH.

HOW KNOW YOU HE LOVES HER?

I HEARD HIM SWEAR HIS AFFECTION.

SO DID I TOO. AND HE SWORE HE WOULD MARRY HER TONIGHT.

...

BUT THAT MY LADY BEATRICE SHOULD KNOW ME, AND NOT KNOW ME! THE PRINCE'S *FOOL*?

I AM *NOT* SO REPUTED!

IT IS THE BITTER DISPOSITION OF *BEATRICE* THAT PUTS THE WORLD INTO HER PERSON AND SO GIVES ME OUT.

WELL, I'LL BE *REVENGED*.

LOOK, HERE SHE COMES.

WILL YOUR GRACE COMMAND ME ANY SERVICE TO THE WORLD'S END?

I WILL FETCH YOU A TOOTHPICK FROM THE FURTHEST INCH OF *ASIA*...

RATHER THAN HOLD THREE WORDS' CONFERENCE WITH THIS *HARPY*! YOU HAVE NO EMPLOYMENT FOR ME?

NONE, BUT TO DESIRE YOUR GOOD COMPANY.

IF HE BE SO, HIS CONCEIT IS FALSE...

THE COUNT IS NEITHER SAD, SICK, MERRY, NOR WELL — BUT SOMETHING OF *JEALOUS* COMPLEXION.

CLAUDIO, I HAVE WOOED IN THY NAME — AND FAIR HERO IS WON. NAME THE DAY OF MARRIAGE AND GOD GIVE THEE JOY!

...

COUNT, TAKE MY DAUGHTER, AND WITH HER MY FORTUNES.

SPEAK, COUNT, 'TIS YOUR CUE.

...

WILL YOU HAVE *ME*, LADY?

...

NO, MY LORD...

UNLESS I MIGHT HAVE ANOTHER FOR WORKING DAYS. YOUR GRACE IS TOO COSTLY TO WEAR EVERY DAY.

TO BE MERRY BEST BECOMES YOU, FOR OUT O' QUESTION, YOU WERE BORN IN A MERRY HOUR.

NO, SURE, MY LORD, MY MOTHER CRIED. BUT THEN THERE WAS A STAR DANCED...

AND UNDER *THAT* WAS I BORN.

AND YOU TOO, GENTLE HERO?

I WILL DO ANY MODEST OFFICE, MY LORD...

TO HELP MY COUSIN TO A GOOD *HUSBAND*.

I WILL TEACH YOU HOW TO HUMOUR YOUR COUSIN THAT SHE FALL IN *LOVE* WITH BENEDICK.

DESPITE HIS QUICK WIT AND QUEASY STOMACH...

HE SHALL FALL IN LOVE WITH *BEATRICE*.

AND I, WITH YOUR TWO HELPS, WILL SO PRACTISE ON BENEDICK THAT...

SO *COVERTLY* THAT NO DISHONESTY SHALL APPEAR IN ME.

SHOW ME BRIEFLY HOW.

I TOLD YOUR LORDSHIP HOW MUCH I AM IN THE FAVOUR OF *MARGARET*, THE WAITING-GENTLEWOMAN TO HERO.

I REMEMBER.

HEAR ME CALL MARGARET "HERO", HEAR MARGARET TERM ME "CLAUDIO".

BRING THEM TO SEE THIS THE VERY NIGHT BEFORE THE INTENDED WEDDING — AND THERE SHALL APPEAR SEEMING TRUTH OF HERO'S *DISLOYALTY*.

BE CUNNING IN WORKING THIS, AND THY FEE IS A THOUSAND DUCATS.

"SIGH NO MORE, LADIES, SIGH NO MORE,

MEN WERE DECEIVERS EVER,

ONE FOOT IN SEA AND ONE ON SHORE,

TO ONE THING CONSTANT NEVER."

A GOOD SONG.

AND AN ILL SINGER, MY LORD.

COUNTERFEIT? THERE WAS NEVER COUNTERFEIT OF PASSION CAME SO NEAR THE *LIFE* OF PASSION AS SHE DISCOVERS IT.

WHY, WHAT EFFECTS OF PASSION SHOWS SHE?

nod nod

WHAT EFFECTS?

BAIT THE HOOK WELL — THIS FISH WILL BITE!

YOU HEARD MY DAUGHTER TELL YOU HOW!

SHE DID INDEED.

YOU AMAZE ME!

I WOULD HAVE THOUGHT HER SPIRIT HAD BEEN *INVINCIBLE* AGAINST ALL ASSAULTS OF AFFECTION.

I WOULD HAVE SWORN IT — ESPECIALLY AGAINST BENEDICK.

...

I WOULD SHE HAD BESTOWED THIS ON ME. I WOULD HAVE MADE HER HALF MYSELF.

...

I PRAY YOU TELL BENEDICK OF IT.

WERE IT GOOD, THINK YOU?

SHE WILL *DIE* IF HE LOVE HER NOT, *DIE* ERE SHE MAKE HER LOVE KNOWN, AND *DIE* RATHER THAN BATE ONE BREATH OF HER ACCUSTOMED CROSSNESS.

IF HE DO NOT DOTE ON HER UPON THIS, I WILL NEVER TRUST MY EXPECTATION.

LET THERE BE THE SAME NET SPREAD FOR HER.

THAT MUST YOUR DAUGHTER AND HER GENTLEWOMEN CARRY.

THE SPORT WILL BE WHEN THEY HOLD ONE OPINION OF THE OTHER'S DOTAGE.

THAT'S THE SCENE THAT I WOULD SEE,

LET US SEND *HER* TO CALL *HIM* IN TO DINNER.

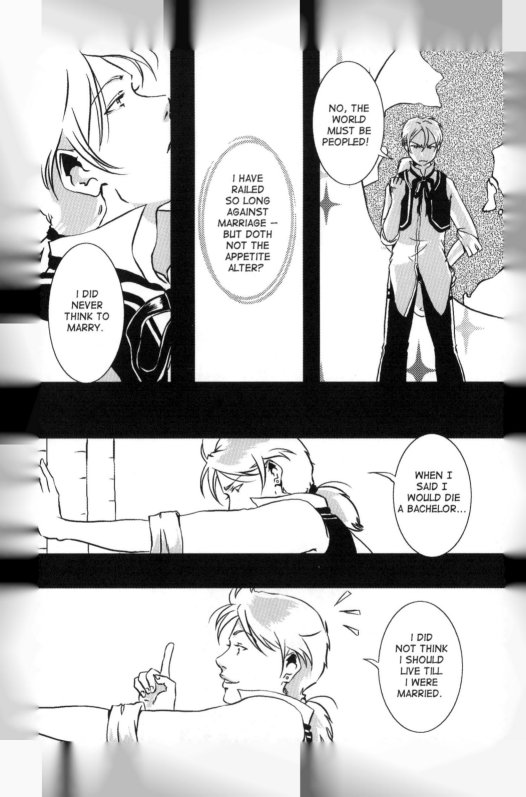

YEA, JUST SO MUCH AS YOU MAY TAKE ON A *KNIFE'S POINT*.

HA!

"AGAINST MY WILL I AM SENT TO BID YOU COME IN TO DINNER."

THERE'S A DOUBLE MEANING IN THAT.

THAT'S AS MUCH AS TO SAY "ANY PAINS THAT I TAKE FOR YOU IS AS EASY AS *THANKS*."

IF I DO NOT TAKE PITY OF HER, I AM A VILLAIN.

BUT SHE WOULD SPELL HIM *BACKWARD*...

Cideneb?

I NEVER YET SAW MAN, HOW WISE, NOBLE, YOUNG, RARELY FEATURED...

...SO TURNS SHE EVERY MAN THE WRONG SIDE OUT.

SUCH *CARPING* IS NOT COMMENDABLE.

BUT WHO DARE *TELL* HER SO?

IF I SHOULD SPEAK, SHE WOULD MOCK ME INTO AIR.

THEREFORE LET BENEDICK CONSUME AWAY IN SIGHS.

IT WERE A BETTER DEATH THAN DIE WITH MOCKS.

YET TELL HER OF IT. HEAR WHAT SHE WILL SAY.

NO, RATHER I WILL GO TO BENEDICK AND COUNSEL HIM TO FIGHT AGAINST HIS PASSION.

I'LL DEVISE SOME HONEST *SLANDERS* TO STAIN MY COUSIN WITH.

HE IS THE *ONLY* MAN OF ITALY —

ALWAYS EXCEPTING MY DEAR CLAUDIO.

CONRAD!

CONRAD, I SAY!

HERE, MAN, I AM AT THY ELBOW.

STAND THEE CLOSE THEN, AND KNOW I HAVE EARNED OF DON JOHN A *THOUSAND DUCATS*.

IS IT POSSIBLE THAT ANY VILLAINY CAN BE SO *DEAR*?

AND THOUGHT THEY *MARGARET* WAS *HERO*?

THE PRINCE, CLAUDIO, AND MY MASTER DON JOHN SAW AFAR OFF IN THE ORCHARD THIS *AMIABLE* ENCOUNTER.

TWO OF THEM DID — THE *PRINCE* AND *CLAUDIO*.

MORAL? NO, BY MY TROTH, I HAVE NO **MORAL** MEANING.

I MEANT PLAIN HOLY-THISTLE.

YOU MAY THINK THAT I THINK YOU ARE IN **LOVE**?

...

grrrrr

NAY, BY'R LADY, I AM NOT SUCH A FOOL!

giggle

giggle

giggle

HOW YOU MAY BE CONVERTED I KNOW NOT...

HELP TO
DRESS ME,
GOOD COZ,
GOOD MEG,
GOOD URSULA...

ahem!

THUD

OUR WATCH, SIR, HAVE INDEED *COMPREHENDED* TWO *AUSPICIOUS* PERSONS...

AND WE WOULD HAVE THEM THIS MORNING EXAMINED BEFORE YOUR LORDSHIP.

Sigh

TAKE THEIR EXAMINATION YOURSELF AND BRING IT ME.

GO GET YOU TO FRANCIS SEACOAL.

I AM NOW IN GREAT HASTE.

BID HIM BRING HIS PEN AND INKHORN TO THE JAIL.

SWEET PRINCE, WHY SPEAK NOT YOU?

WHAT SHOULD I SPEAK?

I STAND DISHONOURED THAT HAVE GONE ABOUT TO LINK MY DEAR FRIEND...

TO A COMMON STALE.

ARE THESE THINGS SPOKEN OR DO I BUT DREAM?

SIR, THEY ARE SPOKEN AND THESE THINGS ARE TRUE.

"TRUE"? O GOD!

WHAT MAN TALKED WITH YOU YESTERNIGHT AT YOUR WINDOW, BETWEEN TWELVE AND ONE?

NOW, IF YOU ARE A MAID, ANSWER THIS.

I TALKED WITH *NO MAN* AT THAT HOUR, MY LORD.

...

MYSELF, MY BROTHER AND THIS GRIEVED COUNT DID SEE HER, HEAR HER, LAST NIGHT TALK WITH A *RUFFIAN* AT HER CHAMBER WINDOW...

WHO HATH CONFESSED THE *VILE ENCOUNTERS* THEY HAVE HAD A THOUSAND TIMES IN SECRET.

FIE, FIE! THEY ARE NOT TO BE NAMED, MY LORD, NOT TO BE SPOKE OF.

I KNOW NONE.

THERE IS SOME STRANGE *MISPRISION* IN THE PRINCES.

LADY, WHAT MAN IS HE YOU ARE ACCUSED OF?

IF THEIR WISDOMS BE MISLED, THE PRACTICE OF IT LIVES IN *JOHN THE BASTARD*, WHOSE SPIRITS TOIL IN *VILLAINIES*.

IF THEY SPEAK TRUTH OF HER, THESE HANDS SHALL TEAR HER.

IF THEY WRONG HER HONOUR, THE PROUDEST OF THEM SHALL HEAR IT.

LET MY COUNSEL SWAY YOU IN THIS CASE.

YOUR DAUGHTER HERE THE PRINCES LEFT FOR DEAD.

LET HER AWHILE BE SECRETLY KEPT IN, AND PUBLISH IT THAT SHE IS DEAD INDEED.

DO ALL RITES THAT APPERTAIN UNTO A BURIAL.

WHAT WILL THIS DO?

THIS WELL CARRIED SHALL ON HER BEHALF CHANGE *SLANDER* TO *REMORSE*. SHE DYING UPON THE INSTANT THAT SHE WAS ACCUSED, SHALL BE PITIED AND EXCUSED OF EVERY HEARER.

SO WILL IT FARE WITH *CLAUDIO*. WHEN HE SHALL HEAR SHE DIED UPON HIS WORDS, THE IDEA OF HER LIFE SHALL SWEETLY CREEP INTO HIS IMAGINATION, MORE FULL OF LIFE THAN WHEN SHE LIVED INDEED.

THEN SHALL HE *MOURN*, BUT IF ALL THIS SORT NOT WELL, YOU MAY CONCEAL HER IN SOME RECLUSIVE AND RELIGIOUS LIFE, OUT OF ALL EYES, TONGUES, MINDS AND INJURIES.

'TIS WELL CONSENTED.

COME, LADY, *DIE TO LIVE.*

BEING THAT I FLOW IN GRIEF, THE SMALLEST TWINE MAY LEAD ME.

THIS WEDDING DAY PERHAPS IS BUT *PROLONGED.*

HAVE PATIENCE AND ENDURE.

SURELY I DO BELIEVE YOUR FAIR COUSIN IS *WRONGED*.

IS THERE ANY WAY TO *SHOW* SUCH FRIENDSHIP?

AH, HOW MUCH MIGHT THE MAN DESERVE OF ME THAT WOULD *RIGHT* HER!

A VERY EVEN WAY, BUT NO SUCH *FRIEND*.

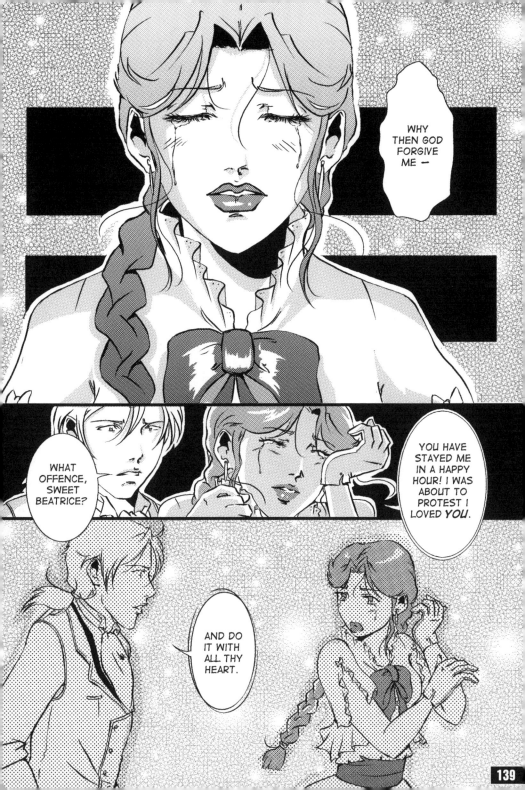

139

BUT MANHOOD IS MELTED INTO *CURTSIES*, VALOUR INTO *COMPLIMENT*...

AND MEN ARE ONLY TURNED INTO *TONGUE*!

I CANNOT BE A MAN WITH WISHING, THEREFORE I WILL DIE A WOMAN WITH GRIEVING.

TARRY, GOOD BEATRICE. BY THIS HAND, I LOVE THEE.

USE IT FOR MY LOVE SOME OTHER WAY THAN *SWEARING* BY IT.

THINK YOU IN YOUR *SOUL* COUNT CLAUDIO HATH WRONGED HERO?

YEA, AS SURE AS I *HAVE* A THOUGHT AND A SOUL.

ENOUGH. I WILL CHALLENGE HIM.

BY THIS HAND, CLAUDIO SHALL RENDER ME A DEAR ACCOUNT.

GO COMFORT YOUR COUSIN. I MUST SAY SHE IS DEAD. FAREWELL.

WHICH ARE THE OFFENDERS THAT ARE TO BE EXAMINED?
WHAT IS YOUR NAME, FRIEND?
BORACHIO.
I AM A GENTLEMAN, SIR, AND MY NAME IS CONRAD.

I PRAY THEE, *PEACE*. THERE WAS NEVER YET PHILOSOPHER THAT COULD ENDURE THE TOOTHACHE PATIENTLY.

YET BEND NOT ALL THE HARM UPON *YOURSELF*.

MAKE THOSE THAT DO *OFFEND* YOU SUFFER TOO.

THERE THOU SPEAK'ST REASON...

KNOW, *CLAUDIO*, THOU HAST SO *WRONGED* MINE INNOCENT CHILD AND ME...

THAT I AM FORCED TO *CHALLENGE* THEE.

THY SLANDER HATH GONE THROUGH HER HEART, AND SHE LIES BURIED WITH HER ANCESTORS –

O, IN A TOMB WHERE *NEVER* SCANDAL SLEPT, SAVE THIS OF HERS, FRAMED BY YOUR *VILLAINY*.

154

155

WELCOME, SIGNIOR, YOU ARE COME TO PART ALMOST A *FRAY*.

WE HAD LIKE TO HAVE HAD OUR TWO NOSES SNAPPED OFF WITH TWO OLD MEN WITHOUT TEETH.

LEONATO AND HIS BROTHER.

IN A FALSE QUARREL THERE IS NO TRUE VALOUR.

I CAME TO SEEK YOU BOTH.

WHAT YOUR WISDOMS COULD NOT DISCOVER, THESE **SHALLOW FOOLS** HAVE BROUGHT TO LIGHT...

WHO IN THE NIGHT OVERHEARD ME CONFESSING HOW DON JOHN YOUR BROTHER...

INCENSED ME TO **SLANDER** THE LADY HERO...

SWEET PRINCE, I HAVE DECEIVED EVEN YOUR VERY EYES.

RUNS NOT THIS SPEECH LIKE IRON THROUGH YOUR BLOOD?

...

I HAVE DRUNK *POISON* WHILES HE UTTERED IT.

BUT DID MY BROTHER SET THEE ON TO THIS?

YEA, AND PAID ME RICHLY FOR THE PRACTICE OF IT.

HE IS COMPOSED OF *TREACHERY*, AND *FLED* HE IS UPON THIS VILLAINY.

SWEET HERO! NOW THY IMAGE DOTH APPEAR IN THE SEMBLANCE THAT I LOVED IT FIRST.

BY THIS TIME OUR SEXTON HATH *REFORMED* SIGNIOR LEONATO OF THE MATTER.

HERE COMES MASTER SIGNIOR LEONATO.

TOMORROW I WILL EXPECT YOUR COMING.

THIS MAN SHALL BE BROUGHT TO *MARGARET*, WHO I BELIEVE WAS PACKED IN ALL THIS WRONG...

HIRED TO IT BY YOUR BROTHER.

NO, BY MY SOUL, SHE KNEW *NOT* WHAT SHE DID WHEN SHE SPOKE TO ME —

BUT ALWAYS HATH BEEN VIRTUOUS.

GO. I DISCHARGE THEE OF THY PRISONER, AND I THANK THEE.

I LEAVE AN ARRANT KNAVE WITH YOUR WORSHIP. I HUMBLY GIVE YOU LEAVE TO DEPART.

FAREWELL, MY LORDS. WE WILL LOOK FOR YOU TOMORROW.

WE WILL NOT FAIL.

TONIGHT I'LL MOURN WITH HERO.

179

NOW TELL ME...

FOR WHICH OF MY *BAD PARTS* DIDST THOU FIRST FALL IN LOVE WITH ME?

FOR THEM *ALL* TOGETHER...

WHICH WILL NOT ADMIT ANY GOOD PART TO INTERMINGLE WITH THEM.

BUT FOR WHICH OF MY *GOOD PARTS* DID YOU FIRST SUFFER LOVE FOR *ME*?

"SUFFER LOVE"? A GOOD EPITHET.

I DO SUFFER LOVE INDEED, FOR I LOVE THEE AGAINST MY WILL.

ALAS, *POOR* HEART!

IF YOU SPITE IT FOR MY SAKE, I WILL SPITE IT FOR YOURS...

FOR I WILL NEVER LOVE THAT WHICH MY FRIEND HATES.

Ha Ha Ho Ha

THOU AND I ARE TOO *WISE* TO WOO PEACEABLY.

MADAM!

YOU MUST COME TO YOUR UNCLE.

IT IS PROVED MY LADY HERO HATH BEEN *FALSELY* ACCUSED, THE PRINCE AND CLAUDIO *MIGHTILY* ABUSED, AND DON JOHN IS THE AUTHOR OF ALL, WHO IS FLED AND GONE!

WILL YOU GO HEAR THIS NEWS, SIGNIOR?

I WILL LIVE IN THY HEART, DIE IN THY LAP, AND BE BURIED IN THY EYES...

AND MOREOVER, I *WILL* GO WITH THEE TO THY UNCLE'S.

YOU KNOW YOUR OFFICE, BROTHER.

YOU MUST BE FATHER TO YOUR BROTHER'S DAUGHTER, AND GIVE HER TO YOUNG CLAUDIO.

WHICH I WILL DO.

Sigh

Skrtch

Skrtch

FRIAR...

I MUST ENTREAT YOUR PAINS, I THINK.

?
?
?
?

TO DO *WHAT*, SIGNIOR?

CLAUDIO, ARE YOU YET DETERMINED TO MARRY WITH MY BROTHER'S DAUGHTER?

CALL HER FORTH, BROTHER. HERE'S THE FRIAR READY.

I'LL HOLD MY MIND, WERE SHE AN ETHIOPE.

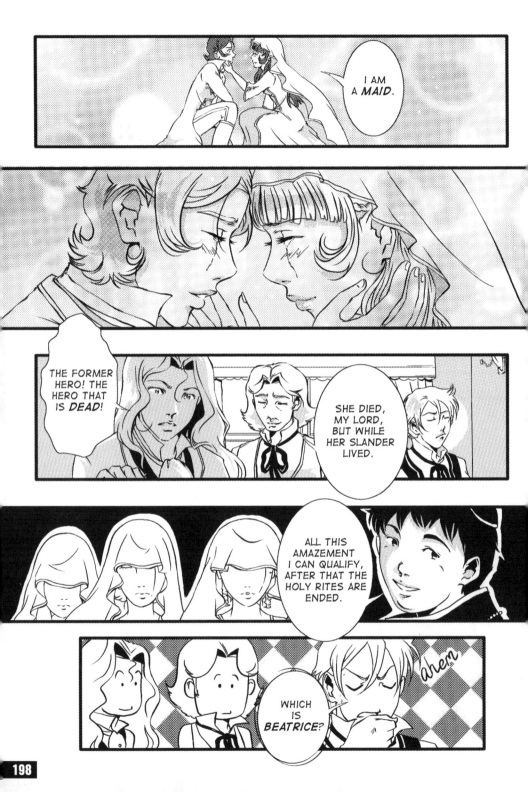

CLAP CLAP

HOW DOST THOU, BENEDICK THE MARRIED MAN?

SINCE I DO PURPOSE TO MARRY, I'LL THINK NOTHING TO ANY PURPOSE THAT THE WORLD CAN SAY AGAINST IT...

I'LL TELL THEE WHAT, PRINCE.

AND THEREFORE NEVER FLOUT AT ME FOR WHAT I HAVE SAID AGAINST IT.

News comes to Leonato, Governor of Messina, of Don Pedro the Prince of Aragon's imminent arrival from the wars in which two brave gentlemen have earned their spurs: Claudio and Benedick. Leonato's niece Beatrice remains unimpressed – she and Benedick are old flames, nowadays exchanging barbed witticisms in their own "merry war". On one thing, though, they are agreed: they are perfectly happy being single. But why is Leonato's daughter (Beatrice's cousin) Hero staying so quiet? Because – as Benedick's merciless teasing reveals – Claudio has fallen hopelessly in love with her. Don Pedro takes more pity on Claudio's shyness: he will pose as Claudio at that evening's masked ball, and woo Hero on Claudio's behalf.

The plan works, Pedro winning Hero's hand for Claudio at the ball – where the mischievous deceptions multiply. Beatrice, pretending not to recognize Benedick, ridicules him to his own (masked) face; while Pedro's villainous half-brother Don John (supported by his cronies Borachio and Conrad) spitefully pretends to mistake Claudio for Benedick, telling him that Pedro is genuinely in love with Hero. This throws Claudio into a fit of jealous rage, only defused when Pedro unites the happy couple. Before Hero and Claudio can marry, however, two more convoluted schemes emerge and play out – one warmly comic, the other chillingly malevolent. Firstly, with Claudio's connivance, Benedick is tricked into believing that Beatrice, for all her spiky hostility, is

actually in love with him; next, with Hero's connivance, Beatrice is identically tricked into believing that Benedick in fact loves her just as deeply. (The trick works, of course, because Benedick and Beatrice discover that they really *are* helplessly in love with each other!) The second plot, implemented by Don John, is altogether more sinister. Using the same stage-managed eavesdropping that brings Benedick and Beatrice together, Borachio drives Claudio and Hero apart: Pedro and Claudio overhear a contrived liaison during which Borachio passionately addresses his girlfriend Margaret (Hero's waiting-gentlewoman) by Hero's name...

Hero is violently jilted at the altar by Claudio; even her father Leonato doubts her honesty; and a black cloud descends over Beatrice and Benedick's newly tender relationship: the first test of his love she sets him is to "kill Claudio". Disaster is finally averted thanks to Friar Francis (the canny priest who believes in Hero's innocence) and Constable Dogberry (the dim policeman who eventually foils Borachio's plot). It is Friar Francis who devises the story's last piece of deception. It is announced that Hero has been "slandered to death by villains": shamed into remorse, Claudio agrees instead to marry the daughter of Leonato's brother, Antonio. But when this mystery bride unveils at the altar, she is of course... Hero herself. As the wedding music strikes up for the two couples, news comes of Don John's capture.

A BRIEF LIFE OF WILLIAM SHAKESPEARE

He learned his craft the hard way. He soon won fame as a playwright with often-staged popular hits.

He and his colleagues formed a stage company, the Lord Chamberlain's Men, which built the famous Globe Theatre. It opened in 1599 but was destroyed by fire in 1613 during a performance of *Henry VIII* which used gunpowder special effects. It was rebuilt in brick the following year.

Shakespeare was a financially successful writer who invested his money wisely in property. In 1597, he bought an enormous house in Stratford, and in 1608 became a shareholder in London's Blackfriars Theatre. He also redeemed the family's honour by acquiring a personal coat of arms.

Shakespeare's birthday is traditionally said to be the 23rd of April – St George's Day, patron saint of England. A good start for England's greatest writer. But that date and even his name are uncertain. He signed his own name in different ways. "Shakespeare" is now the accepted one out of dozens of different versions.

He was born at Stratford-upon-Avon in 1564, and baptized on 26th April. His mother, Mary Arden, was the daughter of a prosperous farmer. His father, John Shakespeare, a glove-maker, was a respected civic figure – and probably also a Catholic. In 1570, just as Will began school, his father was accused of illegal dealings. The family fell into debt and disrepute.

Will attended a local school for eight years. He did not go to university. The next ten years are a blank filled by suppositions. Was he briefly a Latin teacher, a soldier, a sea-faring explorer? Was he prosecuted and whipped for poaching deer?

We do know that in 1582 he married Anne Hathaway, eight years his senior, and three months pregnant. Two more children – twins – were born three years later but, by around 1590, Will had left Stratford to pursue a theatre career in London. Shakespeare's apprenticeship began as an actor and "pen for hire".

Shakespeare wrote over 40 works, including poems, "lost" plays and collaborations, in a career spanning nearly 25 years. He retired to Stratford in 1613, where he died on 23rd April 1616, aged 52, apparently of a fever after a "merry meeting" of drinks with friends. Shakespeare did in fact die on St George's Day! He was buried "full 17 foot deep" in Holy Trinity Church, Stratford, and left an epitaph cursing anyone who dared disturb his bones.

There have been preposterous theories disputing Shakespeare's authorship. Some claim that Sir Francis Bacon (1561–1626), philosopher and Lord Chancellor, was the real author of Shakespeare's plays. Others propose Edward de Vere, Earl of Oxford (1550–1604), or, even more weirdly, Queen Elizabeth I. The implication is that the "real" Shakespeare had to be a university graduate or an aristocrat. Nothing less would do for the world's greatest writer.

Shakespeare is mysteriously hidden behind his work. His life will not tell us what inspired his genius.

MANGA SHAKESPEARE

EDITORIAL

Richard Appignanesi: Text Adaptor

Richard Appignanesi was a founder and co-director of the Writers & Readers Publishing Cooperative and Icon Books where he originated the internationally acclaimed *Introducing* series. His own best-selling titles in the series include *Freud*, *Postmodernism* and *Existentialism*. He is also the author of the fiction trilogy *Italia Perversa* and the novel *Yukio Mishima's Report to the Emperor*. Currently associate editor of the journal *Third Text* and reviews editor of the journal *Futures*, his latest book *What do Existentialists Believe?* was released in 2006.

Nick de Somogyi: Textual Consultant

Nick de Somogyi works as a freelance writer and researcher, as a genealogist at the College of Arms, and as a contributing editor to *New Theatre Quarterly*. He is the founding editor of the *Globe Quartos* series, and was the visiting curator at Shakespeare's Globe, 2003–6. His publications include *Shakespeare's Theatre of War* (1998), *Jokermen and Thieves: Bob Dylan and the Ballad Tradition* (1986), and (from 2001) the *Shakespeare Folios* series for Nick Hern Books. He has also contributed to the Open University (1995), Carlton Television (2000), and BBC Radio 3 and Radio 4.

ARTIST

Emma Vieceli

Emma Vieceli is a professional comic book artist and illustrator from the UK. Since becoming one of the winners of the first Tokyopop Rising Stars of Manga UK and Ireland competition, she has worked with publishers including: SelfMadeHero, Image, Tokyopop and Random House. She is also a key member of independent publisher and manga-styled comic collective, Sweatdrop Studios. This is her second book in the Manga Shakespeare series, after *Hamlet*.

PUBLISHER

SelfMadeHero is a UK-based manga and graphic novel imprint, reinventing some of the most important works of European and world literature. In 2008 SelfMadeHero was named **UK Young Publisher of the Year** at the prestigious British Book Industry Awards.

OTHER SELFMADEHERO TITLES:

EYE CLASSICS: *Nevermore*, *The Picture of Dorian Gray*, *The Trial*, *The Master and Margarita*, *Crime and Punishment*, *Dr. Jekyll and Mr. Hyde.*

SELF MADE HERO

www.selfmadehero.com